StoneSoup

Writing and

D1125549

Editor's Note

In her story "The Bright Yellow," Ella Kate Starzyk describes a character whose world has turned completely yellow: people, food, streets, and stores—all yellow. Her mother takes her to the eye doctor: "After the eye exam, the doctor said I was colorblind, and the only color I could see was yellow. I had a yellow life after that." It is a bizarre premise, and yet a perfect metaphor for the way perspective can alter, and determine, our experiences. When you wake up in a certain mood, suddenly everything you see is "colored" by that mood.

This issue of *Stone Soup* explores perspective and asks: How does our perception shape our experience? The characters in these stories all undergo at least one perspective shift—and it is this shift that drives the action in these stories. These stories serve as a reminder that we are in control of our own narratives, not others. We get to decide whether to think of ourselves as "unique" or "weird," whether to be a victim or an agent, happy or sad. It is an empowering but also scary thought; sometimes it's easier to blame what's out there in the world for our weaknesses than to take responsibility for them.

These stories also remind us: Comparison is the thief of joy. Don't let others steal your joy! Be yourself, unapologetically. And write a story, poem, or personal narrative about what that's like.

Happy reading!

On the cover:
The Fireflies (Watercolor)
Audrey Champness, 12
Green Cove Springs, FL

Director
William Rubel

Managing Editor
Jane Levi

Blog & Special Projects
Sarah Ainsworth

Design
Joe Ewart

Stone Soup (ISSN 0094 579X) is published eleven times per year—monthly, with a combined July/August summer issue. Copyright © 2021 by the Children's Art Foundation–Stone Soup Inc., a 501(c)(3) nonprofit organization located in Santa Cruz, California. All rights reserved.

Thirty-five percent of our subscription price is tax-deductible. Make a donation at Stonesoup.com/donate, and support us by choosing Children's Art Foundation as your Amazon Smile charity.

POSTMASTER: Send address changes to Stone Soup, 126 Otis Street, Santa Cruz, CA 95060. Periodicals postage paid at Santa Cruz, California, and additional offices.

Stone Soup is available in different formats to persons who have trouble seeing or reading the print or online editions. To request the braille edition from the National Library of Congress, call +1 800-424-8567. To request access to the audio edition via the National Federation of the Blind's NFB-NEWSLINE®, call +1 866-504-7300, or visit Nfbnewsline.org.

Submit your stories, poems, art, and letters to the editor via Stonesoup.submittable.com/submit. Subscribe to the print and digital editions at Stonesoup.com. Email questions about your subscription to Subscriptions@stonesoup.com. All other queries via email to Stonesoup@stonesoup.com.

Check us out on social media:

StoneSoup
Contents

Untitled (I) (Canon PowerShot SX530 HS)
Salma Hadi-St. John, 10
Oak Park, IL

The Trials and Tribulations of Swifty Appledoe (Part One)

Swifty Appledoe embarks on a new mission: to become just like the most annoyingly perfect girl in school

By Ariana Kralicek, 12
Auckland, New Zealand

This is the first installation of a novella that we will be publishing in three parts in the April, May, and June 2021 issues of Stone Soup.

"Be yourself; everyone else is already taken."
—Oscar Wilde

Chapter 1

"And that's exactly why you should try Milky's chocolate ice cream!" I conclude, bowing as my excited audience showers me in a standing ovation.

It's Saturday night, and my parents are sitting on our squishy velvet sofa, watching me rehearse for the big advertisement audition coming up in a month-and-a-half's time.

It's important that an actress is very prepared because, as they say, the show must go on.

The TV is blaring softly behind me, showering me in a spotlight effect and bathing the living room in a cool glow.

If I look down, I can see the glassy surface of the coffee table covered in a sea of audition papers, a lone clipboard floating at the surface.

You see, when I grow older I want to become a famous actress. I want to go to the Oscars and win incredible awards, go to the Met Gala and wear a spontaneous-but-stunning outfit, pose and give daring looks to the press as they photograph me, live in a massive—

I can suddenly hear the familiar sound of the Candyland theme song. Obviously an ad break.

The actors' voices start moaning sorrowfully from the TV. I know what they're going to say. I auditioned for this ad but didn't get in.

"Oh no!" a woman cries. "My cat ate my pet bird!"

"Come on!" an old man wails. "My walking stick snapped!"

"Whaahhhh!" A stereotypically bratty toddler, wearing one of those caps with propellers on, shrieks like a hawk. "My cart broke!"

"Don't worry," a familiarly dainty voice serenely assures. "I'll take you to Candyland, where all of your dreams will come true."

In fact, this voice is very familiar. I spin around and stare in utter horror at the TV screen.

A young girl around my age is dressed in a poofy, light-pink fairy costume, a sparkly rainbow belt slapped around her waist. The sleeves of the dress are Cinderella-like, and when you look at her feet, they have been slipped into slim silver high heels. Rainbow ombré fairy wings hide under golden locks of silky hair. She clutches a candy cane wand. But the one thing that stands out to me the most is the rosy, pale complexion of none other than Stella Chichester-Clark.

My mouth hangs open like a door on loose hinges as I gape in envy and anger.

The rest of the ad passes by. The woman adopts a candy bird made out of pink marshmallows. The old man is gifted a candy cane walking stick. Mint-flavored. And the bratty young boy is presented with a candy cart with lollipop wheels. I don't pay much attention otherwise.

Once it has finished, I slowly turn back around to face my parents. They stare at me with sympathetic grimaces.

I can feel jealousy and hate crackling like fire in the center of my torso. Flames shoot through my veins, heating up my body. My head hurts—it feels like a grand piano has fallen from the sky, landed on top of it, and then exploded. My throat tightens. I can't breathe normally. Something's rising up in my throat. *What is happening to me? Am I a dragon in disguise?*

"AAAAAAAAHHHH!" I scream to whatever deity is listening. Maybe the stupid universe can take yet another hint. "AAAAAAAAAAAHHH!"

Then, without thinking, I slam my right hand down onto the coffee table. A sickening crack from the clipboard startles me, but I continue. I swipe at all my audition papers and they soar into the air, fluttering to the carpeted floor.

"Zendaya Appledoe! Stop right there!" my mother gasps in anger.

I stamp, stamp, stamp at the papers, tearing a few pages into shreds. I don't care what happens to them. My life is over once again.

I slump to the floor. My breathing is ragged and sharp. It feels like I'm sucking in spears.

Strong arms hold me close. I sob into my dad's shirt. My mum comes over and joins the hug.

"Don't worry, sweetie," my mother's voice says.

"Listen, you have so many talents that this Stella doesn't have," my dad reassures me.

I don't bother to correct him. Stella is perfect at everything—from appearance and clothes to grades and sports, singing and dancing, acting and making friends. She's annoyingly amazing.

I once heard a rumor that she said her first word only a few weeks after she was born. Adding onto that, her first word was "honorificabilitudinitatibus," a word that appears in one of Shakespeare's plays. It's probably true because she also won the Year Eight Spelling Bee at the age of three. I didn't speak until I was four.

My parents guide me upstairs to bed. A sense of calm has somehow overcome me. It was probably my overdramatic tantrum that did it.

The last thing that I see before I drift off to sleep is Stella dressed in a fairy costume, waving a candy cane wand mockingly at my face.

Chapter 2

The rest of the weekend passes by in dull form. My mind rages with fury at the ad that Stella appeared in.

Finally, but unfortunately, it is Monday. A school day.

When I arrive at school, I can see at least twenty kids outside the main brick building crowding around someone, probably Stella. A few of them walk away every now and then, clutching notebooks and grinning like crazy.

For every one person that leaves, at least three others eagerly join. I gaze in envy.

Soon enough, the large crowd starts heading up the steps to class chattering away, swarming the building like a plague of locusts.

When I walk into class, the bright morning sun is shining through broad windows. Human-shaped silhouettes contrast with the sun's gaze. I shift my focus and sigh grumpily.

There are about half as many people as there were outside, but there are still many jabbering in front of the dozens of bright art projects haphazardly stapled onto the maroon carpeted walls, each with sets of uniquely untidy colored words to label the sections.

Desks are set up in beige clusters,

a few at the front in a row.

"Excuse me," I grunt, maneuvering myself through the crowd to my desk. I feel squished.

My desk, as karma would have it, is right next to Stella's. I don't know what I did wrong to get on its bad side, but whatever it was, it must've been pretty dreadful.

A sporty-looking boy who I think is called Taj leans right on the surface of the tabletop; it nearly topples over. One of the thin, cuboid-like legs scrapes against my left leg as it leans over, leaving a pink mark.

"Hey!" I snap, and he quickly stands up straight, hastily brushing the area that he'd planted himself on.

The crowd eventually subsides, but it's because Stella's posse has strutted into class.

"OMG!" Karen, Stella's copycat, squeals. "I totally saw you last night on TV and you were Ah! May! Zing!"

"I agree," Brooke, her most loyal friend—and also my archnemesis since Year Four—says casually. "I couldn't take my eyes off you."

I can't help but agree with her, although most definitely for a different reason.

Karen fiddles with her short hair, ironically cut into a bob.

Brooke swishes her long black glossy ponytail, millimeters from my eyeballs as Stella gossips to them about all the behind-the-scenes work.

"Excuse me, but your ponytail nearly went into my eyes." I regretfully notify her. Oh no.

She turns around, slapping Karen with her silky mane. Karen blinks her eyes, stupefied.

"So? Suck it up." Her eyes pierce

into mine. I shyly glance away.

"Brooke, you hit Karen by accident," Stella informs Brooke delicately.

"Oh, sorry," Brooke says thoughtfully.

Hang on. How is it okay that when I tell Brooke the same thing, she gets mad, but when Stella says the same thing, she's fine with it?

Just as I begin contemplating it, my teacher, Mrs. Mulberry, breezes into the room.

She's wearing a black T-shirt tucked into a silky skirt with a wave pattern printed on it. Her hazel-brown hair is tied up into a loose bun, secured by a silver scrunchie. A few wisps of hair rest on the edges of her magenta rectangular glasses, framing her deep green eyes.

"Good morning, everyone!" She claps her hands.

"Good morning, Mrs. Mulberry!" the class replies in a hilarious disunity.

"Now," she says. "Have any of you heard of Anne Hathaway, Jennifer Aniston, or Kristen Bell?" Of course everyone in class raises their hands, including me. I'm not too sure, but I think I know where this is going.

"Good!" Mrs. Mulberry smiles. "As you will all know, they are great actresses, and makers of change. And I do believe that we have a future Lily James on our hands." Mrs. Mulberry stares each one of us in the eye, holding an extra-long gaze on Stella.

"As you will know, last night Stella was the star character on the newest Candyland advertisement. I would like everyone to come up and shake her hand. Stella, please come up to the front of the classroom."

Stella swishes up to the front, her golden hair contrasting against the black chalkboard hung up next to the blank whiteboard.

Mrs. Mulberry calls our names, one by one, marking off the roll. I guess she's killing two birds with one stone.

Don't get me wrong, I feel super happy for Stella, but just very, very, very deep down. And by deep down, I mean *deep* down.

Every ad I've tried out for, Stella has always beat me to it. Every A I've gotten, Stella has topped with A++++'s. She has been handed trophy after trophy every year; she wins at least half of the school awards each year, including Student of the Year. They can't give her all of them—but the other half go to the other popular kids anyway.

I don't know when my jealousy of Stella started, but once she started being perfect, the teachers turned a blind eye to her annoyingness. In their eyes, the rest of the class was barely even there anymore.

When it's my turn to go shake her hand, I get out of my seat as quickly as possible. Best to get it over and done with.

I go up to her and shake her hand rapidly, staring down at her classy silver shoes, the same ones from the ad last night. I glance quickly into her eyes, channeling as much annoyance as possible. She just smiles like a hyena about to eat its first meal in a week.

I internally shudder and walk back to my seat, slumping so I can barely see Mrs. Mulberry as she spiels about how we should all try tons of new things this year because there are the Student of the Year Awards at the end of it, blah, blah, blah, so we can be just like Stella, and what a great student Stella is and how hard she works and—

Wait.

Just like Stella?

If I try to be just like Stella, I can be awesome. I can win awards and have loads of friends, do whatever I want and most importantly . . . beat her.

How have I never thought of this before? It's a genius idea.

If I want to become just like her, I'll need to start right now. Take small steps to make a big change.

I mean, it can't be too hard, can it? I can do this.

I know I can.

Chapter 3

Stella plays the violin. I know so because she does a solo performance sometimes at the weekly school assemblies.

So at dinner, I ask my parents a question. This is the start of the first stepping-stone.

"Mum, Dad, can I learn to play the violin?" They give each other confused glances.

"Umm, Swifty, remember that one time you wanted to play the tuba? And how that turned out?" My mum smiles uncertainly.

I sigh as I remember what happened. On the night of the school performance, my lips got stuck in the blowhole of the tuba, and as I was trying to get them out with my hands, I nearly severed my pinky finger off. It actually had to be amputated, which is why I have a scarred stump in the place of the tip of that finger.

So . . . I'm accident prone.

But violins are okay. I mean, of course you have to be careful with the strings, but otherwise they should be fine. Right?

"Mum, I'll be fine with the violin. It doesn't even have a hole!" I moan.

"Okay . . ." She glances again at my dad.

He shrugs, as if to say, "Don't look at me."

"Well, I guess we could sign you up for some classes. How about tomorrow we have a look at places where you can take them?"

"I already know where I want to go!" I reply. "Dux Orchestral Academy!"

I overheard Stella saying that she goes there for classes. The prices are apparently fairly cheap.

"Sure, if you want," my mum says.

Mr. Cello (yes, that is his actual name) sits uncomfortably close to me on a small stool. He's guiding my violin bow quite forcefully. I wouldn't be surprised if the strings snapped. Maybe they could snap him instead of me.

"Now, Swishy—" he mumbles from underneath his tangled Santa Claus beard, which covers his beige tweed suit. It looks like his beard is eating him alive. His beetle-like eyes poke out from underneath thick-rimmed spectacles.

"Swifty," I correct him, putting extra emphasis on the "fty."

Mr. Cello gives me a dark stare, his eyes piercing deep into mine.

"Slicky, it's rude to talk back to an adult. Haven't your parents taught you that?"

"Yes," I mutter. It's obvious I should just agree with whatever he says; me correcting him won't make a difference.

"Anyway," he continues. "From what I've seen so far, your violin playing is very … harsh." Mr. Cello pauses. I can tell he's trying to think over carefully what he wants to say. I don't care how insensitive he sounds as long as I'm better than Stella at this.

"You need to stroke your bow against the strings firmly but gracefully, the way a swan glides through the water. Otherwise you won't be able to make it to the show."

My attention snaps into focus.

"What show?" I ask, blinking nervously.

"The annual concerta, of course. It's only a few weeks away. It is compulsory that all students attend, unless you have appendicitis or something like that."

"When-when is it?" I stutter. *Why am I getting so nervous?*

"Three weeks' time." Mr. Cello replies.

Barbecued sausages! I have barely any time!

"I don't normally let my students do this, but the class ends in five minutes. Take the violin home with you and work on this pattern. It's the foundation for your piece for the night. But for now, play it one more time."

I grip the bow tight, despite Mr. Cello's previous advice. *Gentle but firm. Gentle but firm.* I stroke the bow against the strings, conjuring the feeling of a swan swimming across a shiny, glistening lake. A grating, barbarous sound brings me back to my senses. It sounds like nails on a chalkboard.

I shudder anxiously and close my eyes, slowly lifting one lid only to see Mr. Cello wince. I try again. *SHRRRRIIIIEEEKKK.*

"Stop!" he yells uproariously, before I can go any further. "Class is dismissed! Now go home and practice. Half an hour every day. I pity your neighbors."

I feel a burning shame creep into my head, even though I thought earlier that I didn't care how he delivered his advice. I hurriedly pack up the rented violin, bow, and my new music book and place them into my case, gently slipping that deep into my backpack.

I dolefully open the door, only to be met with the sympathetic face of Stella Chichester-Clark. She's wearing an ironed white blouse tucked into a knee-length black pencil skirt. Her shoes are the kind a child princess would wear: polished black leather with thin buckles. I spot her mother— who surprisingly looks like an older version of Stella—leaning against a burgundy wall wearing running shorts and a very stylish cream-colored fluffy jumper.

"Hey, Swifty!" Stella grins pityingly. "Sounds like you had a rough first class."

Okay, Swifty. Just breathe. Make small talk. Very small talk. And then leave. Fast.

"Umm. Hi, Stella. Fancy seeing you here," I say bashfully.

"I take classes here, silly!" she replies jovially.

Well, yeah. I knew that. Otherwise I wouldn't be here.

"Anyway, some advice: don't take what Mr. Cello says too seriously. For example, when I started taking classes here, I sucked. And now look at me!" she smiles, flicking her golden hair, tied up in a ponytail and held up by a navy blue scrunchie. I smile awkwardly. *Does she mean that I suck?*

Go, go, go, my mind whispers. *Now, Swifty. Make the excuse.*

"Umm, got to go, my mum's waiting. Bye," I mumble shyly.

I tear down the elegant hallway, stripes of gold and red racing through my peripheral vision.

I glance up quickly, only to notice a painting done on the ceiling that looks like it could belong in the Sistine Chapel. *Yikes, this place is posh.*

My foot catches on some loose carpet, and I faceplant into the soft floor. It still hurts, though. My nose feels like it just got KO'd in a boxing match.

I can faintly hear Stella's mum calling, "Are you okay, dear?"

I don't have time to answer. This is so embarrassing. I pick myself up and open the grand wood doors. I can feel something warm and sticky dribbling down my chin.

"Hi, Mum!" I shout as I run out through the grand building. My mum glances up from her phone, then

stares in shock.

"Swifty, what have you done to yourself? You've got a bloody nose!"

Chapter 4

"So, other than the bloody nose, how did your first lesson go?" my dad asks cheekily as we sit around the dinner table eating my favorite food: sushi.

"It was okay, I guess. The teacher kept on getting my name wrong and . . . my violin playing sounded like a constipated train, if that's even a thing."

My dad laughs and shakes his head. "Hah! What did the teacher call you?"

"'Swishy.'" I groan. "Oh, and then 'Slicky.'"

That does it for my dad. He howls with laughter, even though it isn't really that funny. "I have to meet this guy," he wheezes happily.

"Umm, actually, Dad, there's a concert in three weeks' time," I say, stabbing at my food.

"Wow," he replies. "Are you prepared? How many people will be there?"

"The thing is, I'm not sure," I nervously say. "And I'm not even that good yet."

"Hmm," my dad says thoughtfully. "After dinner, why don't you play what you learned today for your mum and me, and we can look at what you can work on. I played the violin back in high school, and I still remember some things."

"But first," my mum says, "we have some exciting news." She glances at Dad anxiously and then bursts, "You're going to have a baby brother!"

Chapter 5

I choke on my food.

It feels like my brain has been lifted from my head. I must be watching a movie; this is all too surreal. My parents and I are the actors, and at the same time I'm watching the whole scene play out from my figurative movie cinema.

I attempt to process what has happened. This isn't real. How is it even possible? I don't want a baby brother. Sure, maybe when I was four and I didn't understand the downsides of having a sibling—but now?

This little brother of mine is going to get in my way heaps. I've overheard my classmates' conversations when they complain about their little brothers, and it doesn't seem fun.

Why would my parents do this to me? Are they bored of me? Do they want to have someone else to hang with when I'm not around? Do family traditions without me?

I only have a few months left with just me and them. That's not a lot if you think about it. Didn't they consider me when making this drastic decision? What if—

"Sweetie, you look a bit shocked," my mum says comfortingly.

"Who wouldn't be?" I mutter, still in a daze.

I stumble off to my room and gently close the door. My mind is racing with thoughts and questions. *Deep breaths, Swifty. Deep breaths.*

Before, it was just about becoming like Stella. Now I also have to impress my parents as well.

I gaze around my lapis-blue room, piles of books and clothing stacked or dumped on any surface I could find, including on the end of my unmade bed. Teddies line my pillow, arms around each other like they're singing a song.

I need to distract myself. I unlatch my violin case and gently take out my bow and violin. I set my music book up on my desk so I can clearly see the notes. I press my bow against the strings and start playing. I don't bother to tune; I don't even know how.

SCCCRREEEECCHHH.

My eardrums feel like they're about to burst, kind of like a pin is popping the center of each stretched bit of skin.

I grit my teeth and try again. Softer this time. *SSSSSSCCRREEEEE.*

I pause halfway. *This isn't going to work. How am I ever going to beat Stella?*

I hear my dad bounding up the steps to my room before slamming open the door.

"SWIFTY!" he yells. He probably thinks I'm mad at him and mum, which I kind of am, but right now I'm mainly in shock.

I give him an innocent but truthful glance. "Dad, I'm just trying to play the violin. I wasn't kidding when I said I was terrible at it."

He softens a bit. "Sorry, Swifty, I thought—never mind. And you're not terrible at the violin, you're just—how do I put this?"

"I'm terrible at the violin?"

My dad gives a small nod and bursts out laughing. "Kiddo, let me help. Hand me the violin."

I pass him the instrument and the bow. He grabs a block with powdery stuff on it that I hadn't noticed before and rubs it gently against the bow HAIR, then puts it away. In one slow, steady motion, he gracefully pulls the bow across the strings. It's not too bad.

"You try and copy what I just did," he says, passing the instrument back over to me. I pull the bow over the strings, sitting my chin on the cool rest. A scratchy, high-pitched sound whines in my ears. I stop playing.

"Ok, so what I can see going wrong is that your fingers are locked against the bow. You need to be flexible with it, like this."

I hand him the bow and he starts waggling it around crazily. I giggle, brushing away frustrated tears I didn't even know I had.

He makes his face go all teacher-like and serious. "As you can see here, only my pinky finger and thumb are bent, not all my fingers. What you were doing was bending all of your fingers and pressing on all the strings quite hard, even though you only needed to press on half of them. Try again, but remember to press on only these strings." He points to a few strings on one side of the violin, then claps his hands in a posh manner. "Now play," my dad says, jokingly sincere.

I do what he asks, and gently stroke the bow against the violin strings. A soft, feathery sound rings out.

OH. MY. GOSH. I did it!

It sounds amazing! My dad is even better than Mr. Cello!

I hear a rustle, and I can see my mum standing at the doorway holding her phone. She grins gleefully. Now that I know, her tummy does look a bit big.

"Mum, you were filming me?!" I gasp.

She nods approvingly. "You're sounding so much better than earlier today," she smiles. "Now show Mr. Cello what you've got."

Chapter 6

Three weeks have passed so quickly, I think to myself as I wait backstage, twisting my knee-length skirt into tight circles around my index finger.

My tummy feels as though thousands of fish are thrashing around inside, having just been caught by a boat lost in a chaotic storm, and my hands are icy cold.

I take a small sip of water from my water bottle, rolling the liquid around on my sapped tongue, and join some kids who are peeking through a small slit in the curtains.

I wish I hadn't. The theater is dim, like backstage, but you can see hundreds of figures moving around in the shadows. I squint my eyes and try to spot my parents, but there are too many people.

I walk away and sit down on an empty crate by some of the amplification gear, clutching the edge of it. I open my violin case and take out my violin, quickly rosining the bow.

I suddenly remember, *I need to get it tuned!* I glance at the clock hanging on the wall in front of me. The show starts at seven—in only ten minutes.

I still have no idea how to tune a violin for some reason, so I head over to a large crowd of small kids cramming around two of the Dux Orchestral teachers, who are assiduously tuning violins, violas, double basses, and cellos.

I join the edge of the crowd and again glance at the time. Five minutes. "Hurry up!" I breathe.

The crowd isn't subsiding, so I head over to another group of teachers, who (surprise surprise) are chatting to Stella. I wait anxiously, tapping my foot in fast beats. But it's too late.

The host, Mr. Cello of course, steps out onto the stage. A bright light shines from under the curtains. The teachers conclude their discussion. One of them spots me.

"Hurry! Go over there so you can line up."

"But—" I stutter.

"No time!" they hiss. "Go and line up!"

I sigh and head over to where all the strings kids are. Stella is at the front, chatting to some snobby-looking girls.

Another teacher calls out names and points to spots in the line. I end up somewhere in the middle.

Time passes slowly yet quickly. The line gradually thins as the scarily sharp voice of Mr. Cello announces new acts. It feels like ages, but the performances seem to last a few seconds at a time in my mixed-up mind. Each time I have to take a step forward in the queue, my anxiety grows.

More terrible thoughts enter my mind. I try to imagine them quickly floating away on clouds, but it's no use. I'm too nervous.

Finally, it's my turn to walk onstage. Mr. Cello announces my name, then walks off. My stomach does a flip. I take small steps to the center of the stage then sit down on a plastic chair. A microphone sits on a stand in front of me.

I stare down at my violin. This is too real.

Way too real.

The sounds I hear from the audience seem to be way louder than normal, and the spotlight shining on the stage is so bright.

Gosh gosh gosh gosh gosh, I think nervously, as pins stab at my core. Just do it.

And then I start to play.

SCRRRREEEEEEEEEE! the violin shrieks. I hear a gasp from some of the audience members. I stop playing and stare down at my violin. *The strings are way too tight, but why? Wouldn't they be loose if I hadn't tuned them yet?* I glance to the side of the stage, but no one is there.

Fear creeps up my spine, a cold wave of sorrow and terror wrapping itself around my head.

Oh. My. Gosh. If this were a nightmare, it would have to be the worst I've experienced. I try to play again, pressing gently on the strings with my bow. Snaps suddenly pierce the air, and I jerk my head back. All of the strings have snapped, leaving harsh pink lines on the back of my hand. I wince. Still, no one comes to help.

I can't just leave the audience awkwardly sitting there, though. I brush away the tears in my eyes, and stare at the violin. It's hollow. Maybe I could tap out a drum beat?

I turn the violin over and start tapping, a beat quickly forming out in my head. I am completely and utterly destroying this beautiful instrument. The wood must be so delicate, but right now it doesn't matter.

I think of the criticizing violin teachers and shudder, but I continue anyway.

The mic amplifies it, giving it an ASMR effect. Hey. This is actually kind of nice. I close my eyes and continue tapping. My beats are loose and free. I like it.

I hear a wolf whistle, and then . . . clapping.

Quiet at first, and then louder. A few more cheers. I keep on improvising for a few more minutes, and then conclude.

An uproarious wave of clapping takes me aback. I smile and wave, and then head offstage. *Was all that for me?*

All I know is that for the rest of the night, I can't stop grinning.

————————————

After the concerta, my parents find me backstage and wrap me in a big hug.

"You were absolutely stupendous!" my dad beams proudly.

My mum scoops me up into another hug, her bump, my baby brother, squishing me extra. "I love you," she mumbles underneath tangles of my long hair. I nestle into her soft arms.

"Swifty, someone wants to talk to you," my dad interrupts.

I stare at a middle-aged man wearing a white ironed shirt and flat black trousers. He has black, rectangular-framed glasses and short, curly brown hair.

"Hello, Swifty. My name is Peter Walker. I am a journalist for the *New Zealand Herald*, and my son actually takes double bass classes here." He shakes my hand. "I saw your violin performance, or should I say drum performance, and it was by far the most unique performance of the night. Could I possibly interview you for an article?"

And that was how I ended up in the news.

Chapter 7

————————————

The Little Drummer Girl
By Peter Walker

Pure talent was unleashed at Dux Orchestral Academy's annual concerta last week when a beginning violinist improvised after the strings on her violin snapped.

Swifty Appledoe, age 10, said that after being unable to get someone to help her tune her violin, she decided to go with it, despite extreme nerves and little knowledge of the instrument.

She recalls: "When the violin strings snapped, there was this overwhelming wave of shock and confusion that hit me really hard. I was looking around, and no one was there to help me. I thought it would be really awkward if I walked offstage without having played anything, so I decided to see what I could do with the [broken] instrument. Somehow, it came naturally to me to just tap along to a beat in my head. I definitely didn't expect the reaction I got!"

There were compliments for Swifty that night from many audience members. Pamela Wong, whose daughter plays the viola, said, "Young Swifty was the star of the show! Such bravery to persist in front of a very large audience. I couldn't have done it myself."

Another, Dagsworth Nickleberry, stated, "Completely different from anything that night. I think she was the most talented one there."

Mr. Darius Cello, Swifty's violin teacher, had less positive things to say: "Swishy should have known how to tune the violin, and her performance was unacceptable."

But Swifty has reacted to that comment, saying that Mr. Cello "had never taught [her] how to do so."

Many other compliments followed, including head teacher and renowned double bassist Martha Charity, who said that Swifty "had displayed courage and musicality in a tricky time."

Swifty has now quit playing the violin and has decided to take up drumming lessons, which she will start soon.

Mrs. Mulberry concludes reading the article and grins at the class, especially me. "Well done, Swifty!" she exclaims.

Chapter 8

I feel great about appearing in an article. Incredible, in fact. Every time I look at the article, it feels like a weight has been lifted off my head and a smile is painted on my face. I feel like I can do anything.

But it's time to take the next stepping-stone. I feel like I could do more, especially with my new achievement! Every time I think about it, my mind flaps away happily.

Anyway, I recently found out that Stella does ballet. This is great, firstly because it takes skill and secondly because I need to impress my parents—and what parent doesn't like their daughter dancing?

But I don't know where Stella takes her classes, so at lunchtime, I reluctantly head over to her clique and stand awkwardly at the edge of the trio. Brooke spies me and sneers. "What do you want, Swishy?"

I grimace at my new nickname. Ever since Mr. Cello called me Swishy in the news article, people have been nicknaming me that. But I don't really care. Swifty isn't even my real name. My real name is Zendaya, but once when I was seven, I ran a race and beat all the fastest boys in my class. Boys being faster than girls is just a stereotype. Still, the name Swifty stuck like superglue.

"I said, what do you want?!" Brooke

sneers again.

I snap back to attention. "Just—c-could I t-t-talk to Stella?" I stammer.

"No, you're not—" Brooke is interrupted by Stella, who says, "Sure!"

She takes me away from her group and says, "Sorry about Brooke. But what do you want?"

Now, Swifty. I stare deep into her ocean-blue eyes and ask, "W-w-where do you t-take ballet c-classes?"

Chapter 9

Peak Stone Ballet Academy is located on what is, in my opinion, a very posh country road. It's a three-story building, which looks similar to the White House, if it were downgraded a fraction, size-wise.

The windows are small and arched like those you would find on a fairytale castle, appearing every meter or so. Wide cobblestone steps lead up to the grand entrance doors, which are painted a soft sky blue. The spherical doorknobs look like they've been coated in gold leaf. I clutch my left hand around the cool doorknob, and, with my mother following behind, step inside.

I'm taking a tryout class here, which is free. It's a good thing, too, because my dad had a look at the prices last night for weekly classes and they're freaky expensive.

I have no idea how rich Stella is, but she must be pretty wealthy to be able to come here. That's why I'm aiming for a beginner's scholarship.

We walk inside the building, which is very classy. The floor is a marble chessboard with faint grey veins running on each tile, and from the ceiling hangs a rather large chandelier.

We make our way to the reception desk, which is also a very white marble, with swirls of gold, grey, and black patterned throughout.

A thin woman, who almost looks like she's been printed onto some kind of card, stands behind it, her face gaunt and pointed, a hawklike nose protruding from the center of it. Her hair has been pulled into an extremely tight black bun, so tight that you can almost hear it screaming in protest. You can see her skin stretching at her eyes and cheeks because of how suffocating it is.

"Name," she states. It sounds like she's got a blocked nose.

"Umm, this is my daughter, Zendaya Appledoe, but she likes to be called Swifty," my mother replies anxiously.

"We don't call our students by nicknames," Hawk Lady sneers as she types into a big computer and scrolls down the screen using a golden mouse. "Ah! Zendaya, it looks like you're in my class. My name is Anita Poof, with a silent 'f.' You may call me Mrs. Poof."

I almost burst out laughing. Anita Poo? The way she said it, it sounded like "I need to poo."

"Follow me." She smiles falsely, and I grab my backpack from my mum, say goodbye to her, and follow Mrs. Poof up a spiral staircase to my first ballet class ever.

She opens a set of polished wooden doors, and we walk into a spacious room.

Large mirrors cover two walls of

the room, a barre cutting through one of them. The ground is made of polished wood planks, and at the back of the room are several girls wearing pink-and-black leotards with soft pink tights. They are busily putting on tiny ballet shoes and eagerly chattering away to each other, getting last sips of water and starting to warm up at the same time.

I notice a slim older boy with dark brown hair in thin black clothes sitting in one corner and tapping something into his phone. He looks lonely.

Mrs. Poof grabs a ruler from a stationary tray right by her and raps it against the door. If I look closely, I can see small dents scattered along it.

"Ladies!" She announces sharply. It sounds like she got rid of whatever was stuck up her hawk nose. "And Pablo." She glances disdainfully at the boy, saying his name like it's a bad word.

The girls stop what they were doing and race over to the barre, Pablo reluctantly following behind.

Pablo earns a spot at the back.

"Move over, Picasso."

"I can't see! Can you go to the back?"

"No! I want to talk to Christina."

"You're squashing me!"

Mrs. Poof raps the door again.

"Ladies! And Pablo. We have a new student joining us. Her name is Zendaya, and she is trying out a class today." Mrs. Poof gestures to me like I'm a doggy dropping. Nice.

At the front of the line, I can see Stella, with Brooke, and Karen right behind her. They glance at me deridingly and then whisper to Stella,

who giggles. I feel my face heat up like I've stuck it in an oven.

"Zendaya! I would like you to run a few laps of the studio to warm yourself up. Then you may join the other girls, and Pablo, at the back of the line."

I look down and drop my bag by the others, then proceed to do a lap of humiliation.

All the other girls seem so slim and perfect; I'm not like that. And being singled out isn't something I like, especially when I'm as visible as the Sky Tower.

Once I've done that, I head over to the barre and join in with the exercises the other girls are already doing.

We start off with pliés.

They look easy, but then I try it.

While the other girls and Pablo sink deep down into a grand plié, I can barely do a demi without lifting my heels up and sticking my back out like a frog about to jump.

"Zendaya! Heels down!" cries Mrs. Poof as she scuttles over and kneels on the hardwood floor. She grips her clawlike fingers around my ankles and starts pushing. It feels like nails are being impaled into my feet.

"Sink lower, lower—that's it!" she exclaims, grunting with exasperation. "Ow" is all I have to say.

It feels like my Achilles tendons are about to snap, and my back is cramping up. Yikes. I can't even believe I'm this stiff.

Finally, Mrs. Poof lets go of my ankles. I sigh with relief. Next, we work on positions.

The other girls can make a 180-degree line with their feet, but if

I try to attempt that I'll probably fall over. Or strain something. Mrs. Poof, once again, corrects my legs, and I feel an excruciatingly tight stretch on the insides of my feet. We do a couple more exercises, both on the barre and on the floor, and then move on to leaps.

Stella goes first. She is graceful and light. Brooke is strong and powerful. Karen is . . . eager.

The rest of the girls, and Pablo, follow. Now it's my turn. Why do I have to be last?

"Remember: stretch your legs!" Mrs. Poof cajoles snobbily. I take a deep breath and then go for it.

My leap is kind of like a large, weighted step. *Thump.*

I land and present.

I smile somewhat confidently, but inside I'm cringing. I think I sounded like an elephant.

The rest of the class continues. We do little routines across the studio floor, *pas de deux* with Pablo, and some more intricate footwork.

While the other girls go *en pointe*, Pablo helps me with my technique, and at long last, it's the end of my first ballet class.

As I'm packing up my things, my mum walks into the studio. Mrs. Poof brings her to a corner of the class. It's a short conversation, but one phrase does stand out to me: "Zendaya simply does not have the ability to continue with ballet."

I feel a rush of shame, but I have to agree: ballet is not meant for me. There are so many rules, like how your feet have to sit in different positions, how you can only do things a certain way, and how you have to hold yourself.

I like some rules, but not a lot. Ballet, for me, has a bit too many.

Once my mum has finished talking to Mrs. Poof, I wave to her and we slowly head home.

That night, we are watching the news when a piece on a hip-hop group comes on.

My attention snaps to the TV screen. All of the dancers' body movements are jagged, but at the same time, flowing. The style is free, and I kind of like it.

So that night I ask my parents, "Can I do hip-hop?"

. . . to be continued in the May 2021 issue of Stone Soup.

A New Nature

Stone Soup Refugee Project

By Ikran Mohamed, 11
Minneapolis, MN; Somalia

I am a new flower in a tree
a unique red bird in a nest full of blue
birds. A fish out of water. I am the
school's newborn. My school is a
new jungle in my head.

Untitled (II) (Canon PowerShot SX530 HS)
Salma Hadi-St. John, 10
Oak Park, IL

Two Poems

By Sadie Smith, 10
Washington, DC

Climbing Treetops

Chittering monkey.
In spring he climbs treetops,
And thinks himself tall.
In winter he lies down
Like the rest of us all.

The Breeze

Luxurious giraffe
Eats the high leaves,
Stretches her neck,
And watches the breeze
As it blows leaves out of even her reach.

The Cookie Jar

A blue cookie jar helps Elsie get through her days

By Isabelle Chapman, 13
Long Branch, NJ

Elsie was obsessed with her cookie jar.

It hadn't started that way. At first, it was practically useless, merely a vehicle for her beloved chocolate chip cookies. But then, even after each cookie had gone, annihilated by the impatient and hungry parents and siblings who shared them, the jar remained. Elsie found it comforting, in a metaphoric sense. In place of a stuffed animal, or something more commonplace to carry around for a girl her age, she even began to bring it around with her, in spite of its excessive weight. She felt that she was sending a clear message to the jar: she appreciated its loyalty, and this was her way of paying it back.

Of course, she couldn't show it to her friends. First of all, they wouldn't understand. And second of all, even beyond the realm of being unable to comprehend her immense attachment to this jar of porcelain, they would make fun of her for it. It's not that they were mean-spirited; they just had a tendency to act without regard for the feelings of the owners of said jars of porcelain.

So, instead of foolishly carrying it around in broad daylight, Elsie kept her jar in her mint-green duffel bag. So as not to arouse suspicion, she put everyday items in there as well: a generously sized water bottle, a keychain to her old house, a keychain to her current house, and the thick cookbook she used to pore over before realizing that the true gift lay not in the cookie but in its jar. For three years—ages eight to eleven—her system had worked seamlessly.

That was, it had worked seamlessly until May 5, 2020.

Stuck at home with her careless, lazy siblings during the quarantine, Elsie never quite realized how much school had offered an escape from home just as much as home had offered an escape from school. But it wasn't all bad. For one thing, she didn't even have to worry about being separated from her cookie jar, and for another, she didn't have to worry about her friends reacting negatively to said cookie jar.

Until May 5, she hadn't even bothered to go outside. Well, she *had* gone outside. She'd gone out for walks, and to ride her bicycle. She just hadn't gone outside with her family, nor had she gone outside to a place

Entrapped (Colored pencil)
Andralyn Yao, 12
West Lafayette, IN

that wasn't her neighborhood. It would have grated on her much more if it hadn't meant a surplus of time with her cookie jar. It was peculiar, because she had presumed that the endless amount of time with the jar would cause a rift between them. After all, she'd only gone off M&Ms after her mom had bought her an endless supply, and only seemed to get bored of *The Office* after she'd seen a whole season in a night (thanks to her cookie-jar-judging friends—they could sometimes be cool). It seemed to Elsie that the more accessible something was, the less enticing it subsequently became.

To her luck, though, it never seemed that way with her cookie jar. She found that she contained the capacity to stare at it for hours upon hours, doing nothing other than pondering its unique existence and inherent kindness (in spite of being an inanimate object). Sometimes, she felt herself choking up when she thought about how it just held all kinds of cookies, no matter their size, quality, or type. The cookie jar did not show a preference for the fancily decorated yet tasteless Christmas cookies her brother insisted on making every year, nor the chocolate chip cookies her little sister liked to bake just as the family ran out of chocolate chips (so, really, they were no-chocolate-chip cookies). It regarded them all as the same. The thought made Elsie feel especially grateful for her beautiful, non-judgmental jar.

Anyway, on May 5, the family

had received masks, two months after they had been ordered. Her parents, delighted they had finally come, decided that they should do something exciting to differentiate the day from others. Elsie's eighth-grade brother, Tom, who was convinced that the coronavirus was simply a conspiracy theory made up by an army of shapeshifting reptiles led by Bill Gates, suggested they forget the masks altogether and go to SkyZone (its closure, he added, was simply propaganda that the reptilian army had promoted). Elsie herself was in favor of staying home and admiring her cookie jar, though her parents quickly vetoed this idea just as it had begun to get traction from her equally apathetic siblings. Her eight-year-old sister, Marsha, had the winning proposal to go to the beach, stating that she thought seashells would make perfectly tasty replacements for chocolate chips.

"Come on now, Elsie. Don't you think you've had enough time with your jar? It'll still be there when you get back," her mother insisted.

Elsie frowned. "Every moment without it is a moment wasted. I'll bring it." Her mother reluctantly agreed. In another family, Elsie's compulsive cookie-jar watching would have drawn more attention from her parents, but given the state of her siblings, she was by far the easiest child.

The beach was beautiful, in spite of the lack of people. It struck Elsie as abnormal, even in such an abnormal time, that there should be nobody else at the beach. She supposed she should consider herself lucky, as her parents hadn't really thought to avoid the crowd; it had just happened that way. But it still felt odd. Beaches weren't meant to be empty, at least not on gorgeous spring days. They were meant to be full of grumbling parents and their wayward children, who begged them to swim with them in the ocean. They were meant to be full of unthoughtful adults who willingly got sunburnt in hopes of a tan, and lifeguards scanning the water for any sign of trouble, and rude customers trying to cut the line to get their Italian ices first. On the one hand, she understood that it would be downright dangerous for a large group of people to gather together on a beach. But on the other hand, beaches without the suffocating crowd of people didn't feel like beaches. It was just weird.

Unfortunately, she was interrupted from her deep thought process by Marsha, who seemed to be holding up a seashell of some sorts in one hand and a dead crab in the other.

"Pay attention! I'll ask you again: which seashell would you prefer to have in the cookies? Tom thinks I should use the beige one," she said, pointing to the actual seashell, "which makes me think I should probably use the blue." She tapped the dead crab. "What do you think, Elsie?"

"Oh, definitely the blue one," Elsie said firmly in the dead crab's direction. "It will make the cookies so much more complex." Only in the aftermath did she wonder if that meant she would be forced to consume the cookies full of dead

crabs. Hopefully, she decided, her parents would inform Marsha of her mistake before it was too late.

Marsha nodded, taking in the new information. "Do you wanna go into the ocean with me?"

Elsie blinked, taken aback. "I'm not sure if we're allowed. I mean, if anyone's been swimming, couldn't we, like, somehow get germs? And isn't it freezing?" She racked her brain, wondering if she should follow her sister.

"Um, well, we could just stare at it," suggested Marsha, who seemed annoyed by Elsie's objections, "and put our feet in. It's fine. Whatever. We don't have to go in if you don't want to," she said.

Finally, Elsie decided it would most likely end up fine. "Alright. We'll go." She grabbed her mint-green duffel bag and quickly yelled to her parents where she was going.

As the two sisters ran eagerly toward the undoubtedly freezing and unforgiving ocean, Elsie, completely focused on the fact that she was about to be drenched in water, completely failed to notice the peculiar, cookie-jar-shaped hole in her duffel bag.

"It's not too cold," noted Marsha, whose feet had almost turned blue. "I mean, it could be colder. In fact, if you think about it, it's kind of disappointingly warm," she added earnestly.

Elsie, meanwhile, looked paralyzed. She did not think of the water as disappointingly warm. She felt as though the water was barely melted from its former state as ice, determined to fix her feet in an eternal state of coldness and pain. She didn't think it was a good idea to be putting her feet in the ocean with COVID-19 on the rise, nor did she think it was ever a good idea to put her feet in the ocean on a non-summer day. How had she gotten there? How had she been so idiotic? Even as she scampered backward, she couldn't shake the dreadful, penetrating feeling in her feet.

"Hey, Elsie. Is that your jar?" Marsha turned and yelled toward her sister.

Elsie looked where Marsha was pointing, and to her absolute shock, she did see her precious cookie jar. It was rolling in the water, its sky-blue paint meshing with the deep blue ocean to form a swirl that seemed to be simultaneously getting covered in sand. *This can't be happening*, she thought, terrified. What would she do without her jar? How would she get through her days?

She knew what her family would say: just get another one. That's what her parents would say, at least—Tom might suggest rescuing it from the Upside Down by searching via the air vents in their ceiling, as he had when she'd lost her teddy bear at six. But why couldn't they just understand that *this* cookie jar was so particular? While Elsie, someone who firmly believed that cookie jars deserved more appreciation, did care for said inanimate objects as a whole, there was something about *this* cookie jar that put otherwise un-shameful cookie jars to shame. It couldn't be replaced. And, watching her sister

half-heartedly duck down and try to touch it, she realized with a sinking feeling that it could not be rescued.

Elsie didn't think she had ever cried so much in her entire life. Maybe as a baby, but babies barely do anything other than cry. She wasn't such a huge crier, anyway. At least not in terms of actual, physical pain. What bothered Elsie more were the little things, like lost cookie jars, the feeling after somebody else takes the last piece of cake, and of course, the final second day of soccer practice (her teammates had found it odd that she chose that day to cause a scene, but they simply didn't understand its significance like she did).

So, it probably made quite a lot of sense that her prized cookie jar's disappearance was such an awful moment for Elsie. She felt helpless because she knew she couldn't go farther into the ocean and save it. She also felt angry because her stupid little sister barely put any effort into grabbing it when she'd had the chance. And more than anything, she felt guilty because if she'd simply left it at home, it would be safe, and none of this would be happening.

"Elsie! Marsha! What's going on? Is everyone alright?" Their mother worriedly came over and wrapped her arms around Elsie, who was still bawling.

"I lost it, Mom. I lost it. I can't believe I lost it. I was never supposed to lose it—"

"Lost what?" Elsie's mom interrupted her, unable to

comprehend what had happened.

Elsie looked up, her bright red face shining even brighter in the sun's light. "My—I lost my c-cookie jar," she finally explained, shaking. She felt so embarrassed to have to say it aloud. How could she lose it? It was the singular thing that she paid attention to.

"It's okay, it's okay," her mother replied gently, hugging her despondent daughter. "It's okay," she murmured again.

To Elsie's shock, though she kept expecting her mother to mutter about a future replacement, she never did. "Shouldn't we get, like, another one?" she asked, not quite sure why the words formed in her mouth, given she'd been so opposed to the prospect only minutes ago.

Elsie's mother sighed. "I think we're done with cookie jars."

Elsie had stopped crying, but the sadness did not subside. "D-done with cookie jars?" she repeated dizzily. The thought made her nauseous. Suddenly, she felt like throwing up. What would she even do without her cookie jar? Watch TV? Do extra homework? Start following weird conspiracy theories? Actually make cookies? Even in her head, it sounded stupid. How could she have been so foolish? It seemed that in her attempt to appreciate and preserve her cookie jar, she'd actually made it even easier to lose it.

"It's just a cookie jar, Elsie," muttered Marsha, who was still standing rather awkwardly near her sister and mother.

"Don't say it's *just* a cookie jar, as though somehow cookie jars are worthless," Elsie snarled in reply. She

didn't understand why nobody took her obsession seriously.

Elsie's mother glared at Marsha pointedly. "Marsha, why don't you join Tom and your father by the blanket? I'll just talk a bit more with Elsie."

Elsie stared out onto the water. She just wanted to erase the day from existence. Not only would she have her beloved cookie jar back, but she'd miss all of the off-putting sights of empty beaches and her sister's disgusting idea to put a dead crab in a chocolate chip cookie.

"It's not fair that this happens to *me*. Tom and Marsha never pay attention to anything, and they never lose anything!" Elsie protested, somewhat childishly for her age.

Her mom nodded thoughtfully. "First of all, Tom and Marsha lose things all the time! Why do you think there are never chocolate chips in the cookies? I always buy them for her, but barely seconds later she loses them." She paused, almost as though she thought it was impressive. She then added, "They're just not nearly as attached to inanimate objects. Anyway, don't you think that it's good for it to be free? I bet your jar is in a much better place."

"You mean in the ocean, getting devoured by sharks? I don't think so, Mom," muttered Elsie, rolling her eyes.

"Why does it matter so much?"

"It just does!" Elsie insisted. "Everybody else gets to have their silly thing, anyway. Marsha makes weird cookies, and Tom likes weird conspiracies, so it's only fair that I should have my weird jar."

Her mom nodded thoughtfully. "I just don't think it's healthy to have something like that. If losing a cookie jar makes you this sad, I can't let you have another one. You're eleven now, Elsie."

Elsie looked down. "I know how old I am."

"Most eleven-year-olds don't bring cookie jars with them everywhere they go," noted her mom. Elsie knew she was right, but she still felt the urge to object. That was only because most eleven-year-olds were idiots and assumed that the cookies were somehow more important than the jar. Besides, how could she be expected to give up something that had been the most significant part of her identity?

Still, she could see her mother's point. She supposed the cookie jar was, after all, an inanimate object. And it was only because of her immense attachment that it had gotten lost in the first place.

After a few minutes of painfully wondering if her days of cookie jars were over, Elsie's mother sighed. "Alright, Elsie. You know what? I'll buy you another cookie jar, and as long as you keep it in the kitchen and promise not to remove it, you can keep it. But if you take it to the beach again, or to your room, or anywhere—"

"Okay! I'll do that!" Elsie burst in eagerly. Any jar was better than no jar, she figured.

She sat down in the sand, throwing it onto her legs until they looked like statues. For the first time in the whole trip, she found that the emptiness of the beach was somewhat special. It was unnerving, yes, but it was unique. And, probably, it would never happen again.

Cabin Fever

By Ella Pierce, 12
Hudson, WI

Today was different.
I noticed the sun
illuminating lands and sea.

I heard every fish jump,
then flop to a smack,
luring the fishers to them.

I saw water droplets bouncing
after my paddle rose up.
They looked and sounded impossible.

I glanced at the treelines,
noticing their exclusive patterns.
Beauty lies in imperfection.

I felt the rippling waves rush beneath my paddleboard.
Flawlessly, they glinted with blurred reflections,
enhancing landscape and light.

Even the air was remarkable,
with a beautiful, timeless flow.
Push and pull, push, push, pull.

The moon became brighter.
An uncapturable light
with stars moving to fit its trance.

Go Bananas (Acrylic)
Adele Stamenov, 10
Bethel Park, PA

The Bright Yellow

A girl wakes up to discover that everything has turned yellow

By Ella Kate Starzyk, 11
Denver, CO

Bright as the sun, a color stands out from the rest. That's yellow. Everywhere I go, I see yellow. I looked in a store in France the other day, and then I said, "Hey, look. The store's all yellow." All the clothes were yellow: yellow boxers, yellow sweaters, and yellow pants. Yellow sandals and dark-yellow mugs with brightly colored cheese painted on the cup for decor. The walls were yellow.

We walked into a yellow café, and my mom ordered a blue cupcake, even though it was yellow to me. It was delicious. The creamy, rich frosting hit my lips, melting in my watering mouth. But the smell—that cupcake, it smelled weird. It smelled very different from a normal yellow lemon cupcake. Mom and I walked out the door after I had eaten everything down to the crumbs. I opened the bulky, hefty door, and a frigid breeze hit me. I stepped outside, onto the yellow pavement, and I narrowed my eyes toward the shops scattered across the street.

Everything on the street was yellow. The shops were yellow. Even though my mom said that the walls were grey, they looked yellow to me.

After hours of shopping, Mom started to get worried to the point where she took me to see the eye doctor. When we walked in, I asked the lady at the front desk why everything was yellow, including everyone in this building. She just took my hand, and we raced through the maze of yellow. We came across a large yellow door labeled "Dr. Johnson." Under the label was a message scrawled, "Come on in!" The woman reached for the door handle and tilted it downward. The door clicked open, revealing the tight room. The woman ushered us inside. The doctor and his room were a garish shade of yellow. I wanted to scream, but I sat down in the chair for the doctor to examine me.

After the eye exam, the doctor said I was colorblind, and the only color I could see was yellow.

I had a yellow life after that. I went home, depressed and let down. I could feel my body go numb. The only thing I could do was sleep. I dreamt in yellow and slept for days to come.

I woke up out of my coma and shuffled to the door. When I opened the massive door, I saw the flowers beginning to grow.

Then, the oddest, most unexpected,

extraordinary thing happened to me. I started to float into the air with my old, chipped yellow boots of lace and velvet. I floated and floated. I flew and flew up into the sky. Luckily, a plane zoomed by, so when the wing passed by, I grabbed it. I suddenly realized that if I jumped off the plane, my shoes could make a soft impact into a sea of yellow.

So that's what I did. I jumped and landed in my mom's arms. It hurt. But at least I was safe and sound. In my mother's yellow arms.

Hands (iPhone XS Max)
Aiyla Syed, 13
Asbury, NJ

Tom Green

Tom Green is very spoiled and lazy—until an accident forces him to change his life

By Zahra Batteh, 10
Washington, DC

Tom Green was very proud to say that he had the best life any human could wish for. He would wake up in his cushiony white bed and then head down his marble staircase, where a delicious breakfast was waiting for him, prepared earlier that morning by his personal chef. If he were to have something involving chocolate, the chocolate would be from Switzerland, where, he believed, the best chocolate came from. If he were to eat something involving berries, the berries would have been freshly picked that morning. Everything had to taste amazing in Tom's house. If there was ever something that didn't meet his taste buds' expectations, it would instantly hit the bottom of his trash can with a small *thud*, and the chef would be off to prepare a new and better dish.

However, this morning was different. When Tom went downstairs to eat his breakfast, there wasn't anything there, except for a note. If he were like his other wealthy friends, he wouldn't have known how to read the note because he and his friends all knew that reading was just a waste of time. There were far more important

things to do out in the world, like making people do what he wanted them to do.

But no, he wasn't like his friends. He knew how to read. The reason for this was because his parents (whom he had banned from his life) had made him go to school when he was young. That being said, it would have been possible for him to get a job earlier because he had an education, but he had forgotten all his math and facts years ago, and the only thing he remembered how to do was read. Now you may be thinking, "If he didn't do any work, where did he get all of his money?" and here is the answer: he threatened his parents by saying that if they didn't give him money, he would reveal to the world that they had killed their last servant, but he wouldn't tell everyone that it was in self-defense.

So every month, they would send him an envelope with huge amounts of money in it (they made their money from their jobs; his mom was a scientist, and his dad was a successful lawyer).

Anyway, back to the note. Tom picked up the note and began to read. Here's what the note said:

Dream Bedroom (Colored pencil)
Rohan Jayakrishnan, 12
Downingtown, PA

Hello Tom. Right now you're probably wondering, "Where is my chef?" and, "Where is my breakfast?" And I bet you're also thinking, "When I find that chef, he is going to be fired!" Well, I hate to break it to you, but there is NO WAY I am going to work for you for free. Now that you've read that part of the note, you are probably thinking, "How is that possible?" I will tell you. You know how you let me swipe your card at the ATM? Well, this morning, I went to get my money, but it said, "Tom Green has no money left to spend." That's when I started to investigate further. I knew you got all of your money from your parents, so I went to their house to see if I could get some answers from them, but I learned something very shocking when I arrived at the house. I also saw a note that said, "Dear Tom. Your parents are dead."

At that point, Tom did a small happy dance and then continued reading.

"They died in a fire that also burnt all of their money. I hope that doesn't affect you at all." That was all the note said. Sorry Tom, your parents are dead. People are already making plans for what to do with your house. Since they were paying for all of "your" stuff, your things are actually their things, and they said in their will that all of their money and houses will go to your younger sister, Emily. You've just lost everything. You have nothing left at all. *Nothing at all.*

Tom didn't know what to do. *This can't really be, can it? This can be solved simply. I just have to go see if my parents are still alive. If they are, everything is fine, but if they aren't . . . well, they can't be dead! Everything is perfectly fine, and this note from the chef is probably fake, just to get me to work more,* he thought to himself. But deep down inside, he knew there was a big chance he had lost everything. In fact, he was so worried about this that he went into his safe to grab all of his remaining fortune that he hadn't yet spent on luxury items! He grabbed his most prized possessions and stuffed them all in the trunk of his shiny white car. Then he drove off to see the people he was praying were still alive.

He parked his car and prepared himself for whatever he was destined to see. He looked up. It seemed as though his heart had stopped beating. When his eyes met the ground, he could see nothing except for ashes. There must have been a fire, which destroyed his parents' house, and his parents must have been in it. He realized that this could only mean one thing: if he wanted to stay alive, he would have to get a job.

Tom woke up. He was sleeping in his new home, a small shed he had bought yesterday, the day he'd found out he had lost everything. He hated everything about this shed. It had the smell of rotten food, the bed was rock hard, there was no personal chef, and so worst of all, he would have to cook his own meals. Tom didn't have that much money left after buying this shed, but it was the only place he could afford, and he wanted to sleep in a home, not a hotel. Since he was running low on money, he would have to start working. He wasn't sure what his job would be. Maybe he could find a job where he would get paid for doing nothing! But he knew that wouldn't work.

He opened his wooden shack door, which gave out a loud creaking noise, and then walked out, hoping that today he would find an easy job opportunity, but it didn't seem like he would, especially in his current location.

One year later . . .

Tom had tried millions of jobs but was continually fired. He worked at a fast-food restaurant but blew up the kitchen, as he didn't know how to cook. Then he tried being a zookeeper, but all the animals escaped when he opened the gates to feed them. And then there was a time when he tried working at a smoothie shop. A guy in a fancy tuxedo and his five-year-old daughter walked in to get smoothies. When Tom tried serving the man his blueberry smoothie, he accidentally tossed it all over his outfit! There had been many failures, but at least he managed to get enough money to buy food.

It was now time for Tom to think of a new job, though, before he ran out of money. He decided he would see if he could be a driver for a ride-share service called Pick-up. After all, he did have a car. When he went for his interview, the Pick-up manager was extremely nice to Tom, which made him feel guilty, for if he had applied

for this job a couple of years ago, he would have acted as if the manager were an annoying fly that he couldn't swat away. The manager seemed to be very fond of Tom, so he let him have the job even though he took a bunch of wrong turns when he was taking the qualification test.

What is about to be said will be as surprising for you as it was for Tom, but he actually began to somewhat enjoy being a Pick-up driver. It was nice talking to other people, which he found himself good at, and he would listen to all their stories. One story changed his life forever.

A man told him about how his friend had died of hunger a few weeks ago because he couldn't afford to buy food. The man said that in the United States, there were over 550,000 people who are homeless, and that more than half of the people in the US have developed the habit of instantly ignoring them. When Tom heard this, he didn't know what to say. For his whole life, he had thought of homeless people on the street as just people who didn't matter. He never really stopped to think that they were people who could do a lot to change the world too, and that they had feelings. Now, he no longer felt that way.

———

Tom hopped into bed and pulled up the sheets. Every night since he had moved into his shack, he had complained about how his bed felt rock hard and how the pillowcase wasn't silk. He had only really thought about himself. Maybe this was because he had grown up in a house with no love or attention from his parents. But now he felt different. This time when he put his head down on the pillow, he didn't complain. Instead of complaining, he reminded himself of how lucky he was to have a place to sleep in, to have money to have food he could eat, and to have access to clean water. He thought it all through and decided he wanted to do something to make sure everyone had a place to sleep and food to eat. He thought of different ways he could help, and then finally thought up a plan.

In the morning, there was no time to eat breakfast. He had to begin his plan. The first step would be presenting his idea to the Pick-up manager. He hopped in his car and drove to the manager's house.

Knock, knock.

Tom knocked on the door, hoping that the manager was there.

The blue door opened, and he found himself face to face with the manager.

"Ah. Hello, Tom!" said the man, in a warm, friendly voice. "Come in!"

"Good morning, sir," responded Tom, with a smile on his face.

"Call me Charles," the man said.

Tom entered the small, but nice, house. He saw a round table with four chairs, and there was also a white couch. The walls and ceiling were all painted in a very light shade of gray, and the floor was made of wood. Charles made a hand gesture for Tom to sit down on the couch. Charles then went and sat beside him.

"So, Tom, what brings you here today?" Charles asked.

"Well, I enjoy being a Pick-up driver because I meet people from all over the world and get to hear their stories. Being a Pick-up driver has completely changed my life, and I believe it could change others' lives too," said Tom. "I thought we could make an organization in Pick-up where we train homeless people to be Pick-up drivers; that way, they can make money and have jobs," Tom went on.

"Tell me more about this plan of yours," said Charles, with a twinkle of curiosity in his eyes.

"I thought that I could be the head of this organization, and we could hire others to give lessons and instruction."

"That sounds amazing!"

Two years later . . .

Tom's Pick-up organization is now called Drive. It has existed for one year and given jobs to 1,681 people. Over the past two years, Tom has had many opportunities to buy a bigger house but has always turned them down because he doesn't need a big house. He has a bed, a sink, water, and food. Instead of buying a new house for himself, he buys houses for people without homes.

Elk

By Cecilia Appel, 13
Tucson, AZ

As the sun rises
A shaggy figure wades through the swirling mist.
His hooves crunch softly in the deep new snow.
He raises his antlered head
And calls to the great winter sky.
It is a promise.
"Have patience!" it says.
"Winter is not eternal!
Spring will return
And cover the forest with her cloak of green.
The life-flame will lick across the valleys
And up the slopes of the distant mountains.
The brooks will laugh once more.
The flowers will open
And tell their dreams to the stars.
It will all come.
Hold fast.
Have strength.
Wait."

Black Lives Matter (Acrylic)
Alexa Zhang, 12
Los Altos, CA

A Small Moment

Allison struggles to accept what her mother tells her: that "different is good"

By Allison Sargent, 11
Rolesville, NC

She combs my hair, carefully untangling each section. My hair is like a fluffy black cloud spreading away from my face. The pointed ends of the comb slide into my hair and out. Like a shovel in the dirt. My mom gives me some of my hair to work on myself. It's thick, coarse, and kinky. I put all my concentration into untangling it, and my mom instructs me on it every single bit of the way.

Mom says, "Your hair is special and unique because it's different from the hair of most people you know."

She says, "Allison, your hair is a beautiful work of art. You know that, right? It makes you special and unique.

"Allison, different is good."

I used to disagree with her. I used to wish my hair were like everyone else's. I used to wish my hair would fall effortlessly down my back. I wished it were straighter and prettier. Besides, doing my hair isn't always fun. I hate how long it takes, and detangling it is horrible! Sometimes we are up until eleven doing my hair.

I don't wash it as often as everyone else because if I do it gets dry. But the worst part is no one seems to understand this! When I say this out loud, they go, "Ew, so you don't shower?!" Which makes me want to say, "No, I shower—I just wear a cap!"

I always know what will happen: My mom with a comb in her hand telling me to come here. The soft pillow that I sit on every time we do my hair. The sweet peppermint-and-mango-smelling creams and moisturizers, My mom's (sometimes) gentle touch. I dip my fingers in the container of hair cream; it feels like dipping my fingers in a cool stream.

"I know." I say to my mom.

But doubt still crawls into my mind like a little ant. I quickly shoo it away, but it's already done its job.

That night, as I lie in bed, more ants crawl in. Soon I have a whole ant hill in my brain. I think of every little thing anyone has ever said to me about my hair. It hurts like little cuts in my head, like little ant bites.

The next morning, Mom asks me how I like my hair. I swallow and say, "I love it!"

As we leave for school, she says her usual line: "Don't let anyone touch your hair! Bye! Have a great day! Love you!"

"Wow!"

"I love your hair!"

"How does it do that, like come out of your head all curly and fluffy and stuff?!"

Then they reach out to touch it like I'm in a petting zoo, like I'm on display.

I don't say anything. I don't do anything. I want to say, "Please don't touch my hair," or, "You're invading my personal space bubble." But I don't. I never say, "My hair is curly because it is."

I try to put it out of my mind, but when my mom picks me up from school, she asks me if anyone said anything about my hair.

"... Well, they did say some stuff." I speak slowly, like I have all the time in the world.

"What did they say?"

"People tried to touch it."

Mom takes a deep breath in and a deep breath out. I don't see her face since her eyes are on the road, but I know she is frowning.

"Don't ever let anybody touch your hair, no matter what. Okay? Your hair is beautiful, and I mean it."

She says this as we stop in front of a bright red stoplight, and I can see the colors reflecting off her glasses like a light show.

I think about what she said until we get home. I go to my room and sit on my bed, twisting the blankets between my fingers. I know I understand what my mom said, so why can't I accept it? I hug my stuffed bunny to my chest and snuggle under the covers. I decide to try to believe what she said, even when it's hard.

This is the Song the World Needs Now

by Nova Macknik-Conde, 8
Brooklyn, NY

Esta es la canción the world needs now
Una canción that sounds like esperanza
Una canción that teaches fuerza
Una canción that makes you feel felicidad
Una canción that smells like salud
Una canción that holds you like amabilidad
Una canción that makes you move like agua
Esta es la canción the world needs now...
Una canción que consuela

Highlights from Stonesoup.com

From Stone Soup Writing Workshop #29: Rhythm, Phrasing, and Cadence

The Writing Challenge
Choose one of these three approaches to your piece of writing:
- Short first sentence.
- Start in the middle with long-ranging sentences that may be held together with the glue of dashes. Don't be overly concerned with perfect grammar on this first pass.
- Write in short sentences. Entirely or mostly.

Dark and Light
By Lina Kim, 11
Weston, FL

The dark was interrupted by a brilliant light
Emitted by stars near the sea.
The moon glowed ever so slightly in the night,
And it seemed like the glow is for me.
I see little white dots shining in the sky,
Looking through the window in my room.
A seagull swoops down near the waves and the tides,
And leads a fish to its doom.
The ocean, stars, seagull, and fish in the night
Show all relations between dark and light.

About the Stone Soup Writing Workshop

The Stone Soup Writing Workshop began in March 2020 during the COVID-19-related school closures. In every session, a *Stone Soup* team member gives a short presentation, and then we all spend half an hour writing something inspired by the week's topic or theme. We leave our sound on so we feel as though we are in a virtual café, writing together in companionable semi-silence! Then, participants are invited to read their work to the group and afterward submit what they wrote to a special writing workshop submissions category. Those submissions are published as part of the workshop report on our blog every week. You can read more workshop pieces, and find information on how to register and join the workshop, at https://stonesoup.com/stone-soup-writing-workshop.

Honor Roll

Welcome to the Stone Soup Honor Roll. Every month, we receive submissions from hundreds of kids from around the world. Unfortunately, we don't have space to publish all the great work we receive. We want to commend some of these talented writers and artists and encourage them to keep creating.

STORIES

Isabel Brown, 11
Phoebe Donovan, 12
Lindsay Gao, 9
Olivia Rhee, 10
Kate Rocha, 12
Sonia Teodorescu, 13

POETRY

Prisha Aswal, 8
Marley Bell, 11
Ayla Bliss, 10
Adam Ganetsky, 13
Stephanie Kim, 9
Elizabeth Ludwin, 13
Ella Kate Starzyk, 11

PERSONAL NARRATIVES

Sabrina Lu, 12

ART

Aaisha Asfiya Habeeb Ibrahim, 6
Lily Power, 8
Madhavan Rao, 5
Anna Weinberg, 11
Grace Williams, 13

  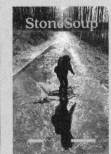
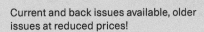

CPSIA information can be obtained
at www.ICGtesting.com
Printed in the USA
JSHW030315090321
12373JS00001B/1